Clumsy Eagle

Level 6F

Written by Melanie Hamm
Illustrated by Nicola Anderson
Reading Consultant: Betty Franchi

About Phonics

Spoken English uses more than 40 speech sounds. Each sound is called a *phoneme*. Some phonemes relate to a single letter (d-o-g) and others to combinations of letters (sh-ar-p). When a phoneme is written down, it is called a *grapheme*. Teaching these sounds, matching them to their written form, and sounding out words for reading is the basis of phonics.

Early phonics instruction gives children the tools to sound out, blend, and say the words without having to rely on memory or guesswork. This instruction gives children the confidence and ability to read unfamiliar words, helping them progress toward independent reading.

About the Consultant

Betty Franchi is an American educator with a Bachelor's Degree in Elementary and Middle Education as well as a Master's Degree in Special Education. Betty holds a National Boards for Professional Teaching Standards certification. Throughout her 24 years as a teacher, she has studied and developed an expertise in Phonetic Awareness and has implemented phonetic strategies, teaching many young children to read, including students with special needs.

Reading tips

This book focuses on three sounds made with the letters
ea; (*ē*) as in **ea**t, (*ĕ*) as in br**ea**d, and (*ā*) as in br**ea**k.

Tricky and/or new words in this book

Any words in bold may have unusual spellings
or are new and have not yet been introduced.

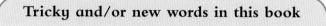

> **Tricky and/or new words in this book**
>
> **mother   two   one   goes
> brother   learn   through
> because**

Extra ways to have fun with this book

After the readers have read the story, ask them
questions about what they have just read.

*Can you remember three words that contain
the different sounds shown by the letters* ea?
Who did Clumsy Eagle land on when he tripped at the beach?

I'm sorry but I can't
give my seal of approval
to Clumsy Eagle.

A Pronunciation Guide

This grid contains the sounds used in the
stories in levels 4, 5, and 6 and a guide
on how to say them.

/ă/ as in pat	/ā/ as in pay	/âr/ as in care	/ä/ as in father
/b/ as in bib	/ch/ as in church	/d/ as in deed/ milled	/ĕ/ as in pet
/ē/ as in bee	/f/ as in fife/ phase/ rough	/g/ as in gag	/h/ as in hat
/hw/ as in which	/ĭ/ as in pit	/ī/ as in pie/ by	/îr/ as in pier
/j/ as in judge	/k/ as in kick/ cat/ pique	/l/ as in lid/ needle (nēd'l)	/m/ as in mom
/n/ as in no/ sudden (sŭd'n)	/ng/ as in thing	/ŏ/ as in pot	/ō/ as in toe
/ô/ as in caught/ paw/ for/ horrid/ hoarse	/oi/ as in noise	/o͝o/ as in took	/ū/ as in cute

/ou/ as in **ou**t	/p/ as in **p**o**p**	/r/ as in **r**oar	/s/ as in **s**au**ce**
/sh/ as in **sh**ip/ di**sh**	/t/ as in **t**igh**t**/ stopp**ed**	/th/ as in **th**in	/th/ as in **th**is
/ŭ/ as in **c**u**t**	/ûr/ as in **ur**ge/ t**er**m/ f**ir**m/ w**or**d/ h**ear**d	/v/ as in **v**al**ve**	/w/ as in **w**ith
/y/ as in **y**es	/z/ as in **z**ebra/ **x**ylem	/zh/ as in vi**si**on/ plea**s**ure/ gara**g**e/	/ə/ as in **a**bout/ it**e**m/ edibl**e**/ gall**o**p/ circ**u**s
/ər/ as in butt**er**			

Be careful not to add an /uh/ sound to /s/, /t/, /p/, /c/, /h/, /r/, /m/, /d/, /g/, /l/, /f/ and /b/. For example, say /ff/ not /fuh/ and /sss/ not /suh/.

Mother Eagle has
three little eaglets.

Two of them are neat and careful. **One** of them is clumsy.

Clumsy Eagle wreaks havoc wherever he **goes**.

On the beach, he trips and
lands on an unsuspecting seal,
who is not very pleased.

At home, he tears a hole in the nest and he knocks a meal right out of his sister's beak.

"I'm sorry," he says.
"I meant to be more careful."

He tries to clean up the
mess as he treads on his
brother's head.

"I'm sorry," he says.
"I meant to be
more careful."

His mother surveys the nest
and glances at the beach.

"Oh, Clumsy Eagle," she sighs.
"I dread the day you **learn** to fly."

The big day gets
nearer and nearer.
The weather is ideal.

The sun is gleaming. Clumsy Eagle
perches shakily on a post and
watches the breaking waves.

"Please be careful!" his mother entreats. "Look straight ahead," squeal his siblings.

"Not in my direction,"
pleads the fearful seal.

Clumsy Eagle takes a deep breath. He spreads his wings.

He reaches up to
the sky and leaps.

Wow! Clumsy Eagle weaves
through the clouds and
swoops over the beach.

The onlookers beam with delight **because** Clumsy Eagle is great at flying.

OVER **48** TITLES IN SIX LEVELS
Betty Franchi recommends...

Some titles from Level 4

The Circus Mice — 978 1 84898 783 8

Monster's Night — 978 1 84898 784 5

Jemima The Spy — 978 1 84898 785 2

Some titles from Level 5

The Gigantic Bear — 978 1 84898 787 6

Celebrity Celia — 978 1 84898 788 3

The Cemetery Dance — 978 1 84898 789 0

Other titles to enjoy from Level 6

Hugh is New — 978 1 84898 791 3

Owen the Astronaut — 978 1 84898 794 4

Bad Zombie Movie — 978 1 84898 793 7

An Hachette Company
First published in the United States by TickTock, an imprint of Octopus Publishing Group.
www.octopusbooksusa.com

Copyright © Octopus Publishing Group Ltd 2013

Distributed in the US by
Hachette Book Group USA
237 Park Avenue, New York NY 10017, USA

Distributed in Canada by
Canadian Manda Group
165 Dufferin Street, Toronto, Ontario, Canada M6K 3H6

ISBN 978 1 84898 792 0

Printed and bound in China
10 9 8 7 6 5 4 3 2 1